Ernest & Celestine
Merry Christmas

Gabrielle Vincent

Catnip

Ernest, when's Christmas? In six days.

But . . . you promised me a party with all my friends.

We can't afford it – come along!

But Ernest, you don't need money to have a Christmas party!

What about a tree and presents and cakes and music and candles and all the rest, eh?

Ernest, I *know* we don't need money for our party!
It's too cold to think about Christmas parties.

We'll go and find a
Christmas tree!

You can play the violin
and we'll dance
and sing.

And you can make cakes,
biscuits, fruit punch, hot
chocolate and that's that!

For presents we'll draw pictures and
make collages and cut-outs . . .

. . . and hats
and stars . . .

. . . and garlands
and streamers.

Say yes, Ernest, say yes!
No means no! Not this year.

But you promised . . .

Well, all right, yes, I did promise. Fine.

I can't believe you forgot your promise, Ernest!

Come and see all my lovely presents.

Coming . . . I'm just baking the cakes . . . hey, Celestine, we need to find more crockery!

Over there, Ernest! I can see some cups and plates!

Hmm, and there's just what I need for my costume . . .

Not bad!

And her dress! Ha!

Write it neatly, Celestine:

*A big Christmas party at
Ernest and Celestine's house.
Bring your recorders, drums,
candles and party hats.
The more the merrier!*

What sort of a party is this?!

. . . and that's for you.

You call *that* a Christmas tree?

Fake baubles, fake garlands, no music . . .

Don't listen to him, Celestine,
we think it's all beautiful.

Ernest, come and see.   Ernest! Ernest?   Where are you, Ernest?

Father Christmas is here!

I've lost Ernest!

Celestine doesn't recognize him –
she thinks it's the *real* Father Christmas.

Look, Celestine.

It's Ernest!

Wa-hoo!

Louder!

Go for it, Ernest!

Keep singing, Celestine!

A story,
tell us a story!

Once upon a time, in a land far away . . .

That was the best
party ever, Ernest . . .

. . . are you still cross with
me, Celestine? It was a brilliant
party, I think. Can I come
again next year?

He wants to come next year?!

I can't wait for next year's party, Ernest!

Let's quieten down now, Celestine . . .

Oh Christmas tree,
oh Christmas tree . . .

CATNIP BOOKS
Published by Catnip Publishing Ltd
Quality Court
off Chancery Lane
London WC2A 1HR

English translation © Catnip Publishing Ltd
Translation: Sam Alexander

This edition first published 2013
1 3 5 7 9 10 8 6 4 2

© 2003 Casterman, Bruxelles

The moral right of the author/illustrator has been asserted
'Ernest & Celestine' series font used with permission from STUDIOCANAL Ltd.

A CIP catalogue for this book is available from the British Library

ISBN 978-1-84647-173-5

Printed in Italy

www.catnippublishing.co.uk